To Actan

Aim for

the Stars

♡ Sheleen Lepar

For my three daughters,
Shannon, Sheleen, and Alicia,
and all children who love storytime.

Happy Bus

Written by Helene Pam
Illustrated by Sheleen Lepar

There once was a
handsome, young bus.

When the bus came out of the garage, he heard that his job would be to take children to and from school every day.

Oh no, thought the bus. How awful!

All those naughty children making a terrible racket every day. Imagine how sticky my beautiful seats will be, and all those ugly candy wrappers lying on my nice, clean floor.

What am I going to do?

For the first few months he was a
VERY UNHAPPY BUS.

The children made him cringe with their noise,
there were candy wrappers everywhere,
and oh how sticky his beautiful seats were.

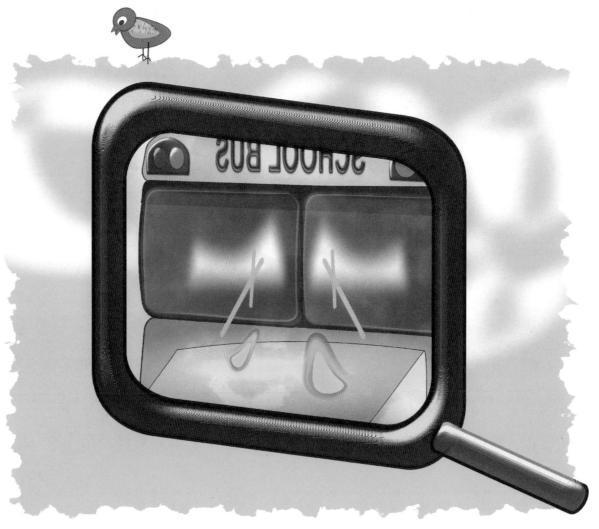

He had to think of something to do.

One day, driving down the long,
  winding road to school,
the noise was louder than usual, and
the children, instead of sitting in their seats,
were running up and down the aisle wildly.

THE BUS HAD HAD ENOUGH.

He pulled over to the side of the road,
  and he stopped.

Can't a bird get some peace around here?

"What's happening?" shouted the children as they climbed out of the bus. "Why has the bus stopped?"

The children stared at
each other in surprise.
"You can speak?"
they asked.

Surprise!

"Yes I can," answered the bus,
"and I won't take you to school any more
because you don't know how to behave.

"You make my seats **sticky**,
leave candy wrappers **everywhere,**
and give me a terrible ache in my engine
with **all your noise.** I was once a clean,
handsome bus, but look at me now."

"But it takes soooo long to get to school,
and we get soooo bored," whined the children.

"I can solve that," said the bus.
"If you keep my secret that I can talk
and make sure I'm clean and tidy then
I'll tell you a different story every bus ride."

"We promise," they said as they jumped back into the bus.

They sat very quietly as they listened to the bus tell them many wonderful stories.

From that day on, the children couldn't wait to ride the bus each day.

The children kept the bus' secret, and the bus kept his promise and told them stories for many, many years.

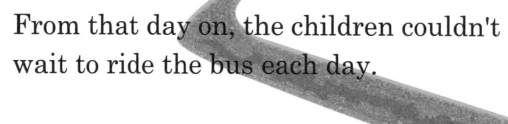

The children grew to love the bus,
and the bus loved the children too.
The bus was filled with such joy
that the children named him

HAPPY BUS.

One morning, the children were waiting
at the bus stop for Happy Bus to pick them up.

CHOG, CHOG, CHOG went his old engine
as he slowly climbed up the hill.
His brakes *SQUEEEEAAAKKED*
as he stopped, and he gave a big **YAWWWWN**.

Many years had gone by since his first story,
and he was now very, very old.

"Good morning, Happy Bus," shouted the children as they climbed up the stairs.

"Good morning, my friends," said Happy Bus. "Jump in quickly, it takes me a long time to get to school nowadays."

The children waited patiently for Happy Bus to complete his route collecting all the children. At last they were on their way.

"Do you have a story to tell us today?" asked the children.

"I'm afraid not," said Happy Bus.
"Today I have some very sad news for you. This morning I heard that a new bus is coming to take my place. They have decided to retire me to a scrap yard."

"What is a scrap yard?" asked the children.

"It's a place where old buses and cars are brought to be taken apart," said the bus sadly. "I know I'm old, rusty, and leak all over, but I don't want to go to a scrap yard.

"What am I going to do?"

"Oh Happy Bus, we'll find a way to keep you.
We'll never let anyone take you away,"
they cried.

The children worked very hard that afternoon going to every house in the town.
They asked everyone to think of a way they could keep the bus.

Most people agreed that the bus was too old to get the children to school on time, but they realized how much the children loved the bus.

They decided to hold a meeting to see what could be done.

After much debate, they found **the perfect answer.**

The children ran outside to tell Happy Bus the good news.

He would live in the park where the children could play with him every day.

He was a **VERY HAPPY BUS**.

They all jumped into Happy Bus,
and with the whole town cheering,
they drove off down the street towards the park.

Happy Bus was well
looked after in the park.
He was painted every year and
felt happy, handsome, and cared for.

Although he was an old bus, he was never lonely because he was always surrounded by children who loved him.

Thank you for reading Happy Bus.

 To learn more about this book and other projects by the author and the artist, follow Purple Splash Studios on Facebook.

ISBN 13: 978-1496120366
ISBN 10: 1496120361

Mother
(Author)
♥

♥
Daughter
(Artist)

About the Author and Artist

Helene Pam lives in Cape Town, South Africa with her Labrador, Kai. While bringing up her three daughters, she developed a passion for storytelling and wrote many heartwarming children's stories.

Her daughter, Sheleen Lepar, lives in Seattle with her husband and daughter and has always had a love for art.

Together this mother-daughter team are working on several children's books with important life lessons.

Made in the USA
San Bernardino, CA
01 April 2014